TIME FOR BED

Mem Fox

TIME FOR BED

ILLUSTRATED BY

Jane Dyer

Houghton Mifflin Harcourt
Boston   New York

Houghton Mifflin Harcourt Publishing Company
222 Berkeley Street
Boston, MA 02116
Manufactured in China
LEO 10 9 8 7 6 5 4 3 2
4500587121

ISBN 978-0-544-53163-5

For Allyn and Louise,
because this book needs two more stars
—M.F.

And for Barry,
because this book needs a bear
—J.D.

It's time for bed, little mouse, little mouse,
Darkness is falling all over the house.

It's time for bed, little goose, little goose,
The stars are out and on the loose.

It's time for bed, little cat, little cat,
So snuggle in tight, that's right, like that.

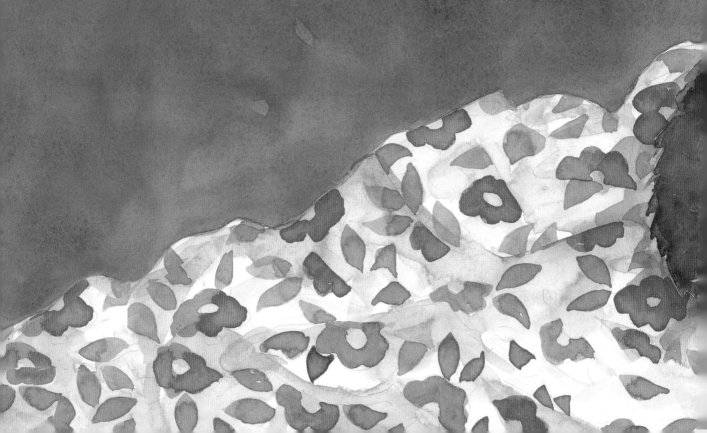

It's time for bed, little calf, little calf,
What happened today that made you laugh?

It's time for bed, little foal, little foal,
I'll whisper a secret, but don't tell a soul.

It's time for bed, little fish, little fish,
So hold your breath and make a wish.

It's time for bed, little sheep, little sheep,
The whole wide world is going to sleep.

It's time to sleep, little bird, little bird,
So close your eyes, not another word.

It's time to sleep, little bee, little bee,
Yes, I love you and you love me.

It's time to sleep, little snake, little snake,
Good gracious me, you're still awake!

It's time to sleep, little pup, little pup,
If you don't sleep soon the sun will be up!

It's time to sleep, little deer, little deer,
The very last kiss is almost here.

The stars on high are shining bright—
Sweet dreams, my darling, sleep well . . .

good night!

Everywhere Babies

SUSAN MEYERS

ILLUSTRATED BY MARLA FRAZEE

Houghton Mifflin Harcourt
Boston   New York

Houghton Mifflin Harcourt Publishing Company
222 Berkeley Street
Boston, MA 02116
Manufactured in China
LEO
4500587121

ISBN 978-0-544-53162-8

For Dylan and Trevor,
grandest of babies

—S.M.

With love for Graham, Reed,
and James—every day, everywhere

—M.F.

Every day, everywhere,

fat babies,

thin babies,

small babies,

tall babies,

babies are born~

winter and spring babies,   summer and fall babies.

Every day, everywhere,

on their cheeks,

on their ears,

their fingers,

their nose,

babies are kissed~

on the top of their head,

on their tummy,

their toes.

Every day, everywhere,

in diapers and T-shirts, in buntings and sleepers,

babies are dressed~

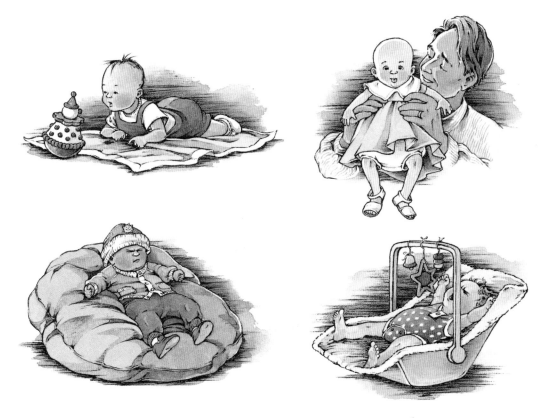

in playsuits and dresses, in sweaters and creepers.

Every day, everywhere,

by bottle,
by breast,
with cups,
and with
spoons,

babies are fed~

with milk,
and then
cereal,
carrots,
and
prunes.

Every day, everywhere,

in cradles, in chairs,

at nap time and night,

babies are rocked~

by friends and relations

who cuddle them tight.

Every day, everywhere,

in backpacks,

in front packs,

in slings,

and in strollers,

babies are carried~

in car seats,

and bike seats,

and on Daddy's shoulders.

Every day, everywhere,

they cry and they squeal,

they giggle, they coo,

babies make noise~

they clap their hands, too.

they bang and they splash,

Every day, everywhere,

rattles, and tops, and books that won't tear,

babies like toys~

old pots and pans, and a fuzzy brown bear.

Every day, everywhere,

peek-a-boo,

pat-a-cake,

this-little-piggy,

babies play games~

ride-a-horse,

roll-the-ball,

jiggety-jiggy.

Every day, everywhere,

with a puppy,   a kitten,   a goldfish,   a bunny,

babies make friends~

with young people,   old people,   anyone funny.

Every day, everywhere,

forward and backward,

on bottoms and knees,

babies are crawling~

wherever they please.

upstairs and downstairs,

Every day, everywhere,

one step, another, they fall down and then…

babies are walking~

pick themselves up and try it again.

Every day, everywhere,

they can run,

they can jump,

they can slide,

they can swing,

babies are growing~

they can dig,

they can climb,

they can talk,

they can sing.

Every day, everywhere,

for traveling so far,

for trying so hard,

babies are loved~

for being so wonderful…

… just as they are!

Ten Little FINGERS
and Ten Little TOES

MEM FOX

HELEN OXENBURY

Houghton Mifflin Harcourt Publishing Company

222 Berkeley Street

Boston, MA 02116

Manufactured in China

LEO

4500587121

ISBN 978-0-544-53165-9

For Helena, who teaches them all

—M.F.

For all the babies of the world

—H.O.

There was one little baby
who was born far away.

And another who was born
on the very next day.

And both of these babies,

as everyone knows,

had ten little fingers

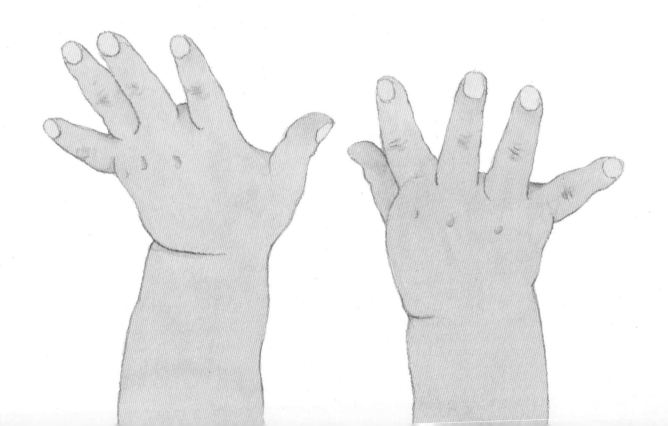

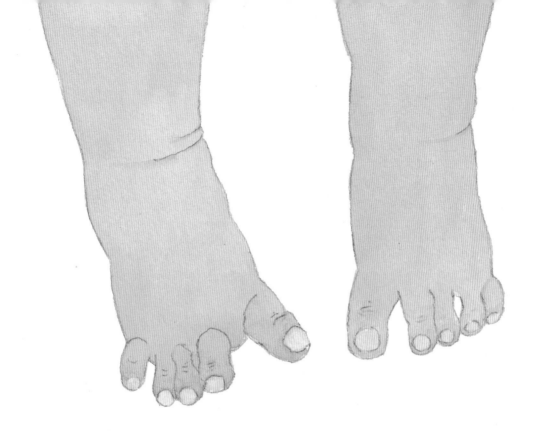

and ten little toes.

There was one little baby who was born in a town.

And another who was wrapped in an eiderdown.

And both of these babies,

as everyone knows,

had ten little fingers

and ten little toes.

There was one little baby
who was born in the hills.

And another who suffered from sneezes and chills.

And both of these babies,

as everyone knows,

had ten little fingers

and ten little toes.

There was one little baby who was born on the ice.

And another in a tent, who was just as nice.

And both of these babies,

as everyone knows,

had ten little fingers

and ten little toes.

But the next baby born was truly divine,
a sweet little child who was mine, all mine.

And this little baby,

as everyone knows,

has ten little fingers,

ten little toes,

and three little kisses

on the tip of its nose.